AKORTA THE ALL-SEEING APE

BY ADAM BLADE

ORCHARD

With special thanks to Tabitha Jones

www.beastquest.co.uk

ORCHARD BOOKS
First published in Great Britain in 2020 by The Watts Publishing Group
1 3 5 7 9 10 8 6 4 2

A CIP catalogue record for this book is available from the British Library.

ISBN 978 1 40836 137 5

Printed in Great Britain

The paper and board used in this book are made from wood from responsible sources

Orchard Books
An imprint of Hachette Children's Group
Part of The Watts Publishing Group Limited
Carmelite House, 50 Victoria Embankment, London EC4Y 0DZ

An Hachette UK Company
www.hachette.co.uk
www.hachettechildrens.co.uk

Welcome to the world of Beast Quest!

Tom was once an ordinary village boy, until he travelled to the City, met King Hugo and discovered his destiny. Now he is the Master of the Beasts, sworn to defend Avantia and its people against Evil. Tom draws on the might of the magical Golden Armour, and is protected by powerful tokens granted to him by the Good Beasts of Avantia. Together with his loyal companion Elenna, Tom is always ready to visit new lands and tackle the enemies of the realm.

While there's blood in his veins, Tom will never give up the Quest...

THE LABYRINTH JUNGLE
THE PEAKS OF DESPAIR

DANGER
DEATH
ZARGON'S
PRISON
MOAT OF
VAKUNDA

There are special gold coins to collect in this book. You will earn one coin for every chapter you read.

Find out what to do with your coins at the end of the book.

CONTENTS

When my aunt Aroha left Tangala to marry King Hugo of Avantia, I thought I could rule this kingdom. I wanted to make her proud, to protect the country's borders and keep my people safe.

I have failed. The sorcerer who took me claims to be hundreds of years old. He says he will not kill me, if my aunt does the right thing. It's the Jewels of Tangala that he wants. A simple swap – me for the magical stones. But if Aroha delivers them, the results will be far worse than one death. All Tangala will be in peril. My only hope is that my aunt has some other plan, some way to rescue me, but save the kingdom too.

She will need brave heroes at her side if she is to succeed.

Rotu

Regent of Tangala, and nephew to the queen.

WOUNDED WARRIOR

Tom sat on a low stone wall in Daltec's apothecary garden, the sun on his back and the sweet scent of herbs and flowers all around him.

Nearby, Daltec picked tiny blue leaves from a woody shrub and dropped them into a pouch at his belt. "That should be enough to fix

Captain Harkman's back," he said, straightening up.

A little further along the flowerbed, Elenna leaned towards a purple rose with velvety-looking petals. "These flowers smell amazing!" she said, closing her eyes and taking a long sniff. "Almost like...biscuits baking."

"Careful!" Daltec said. "That's a Gorgonian rose."

Elenna took another sniff, but with a jolt of horror Tom saw the rose's petals peel apart, revealing white, human-like teeth. "Look out!" he cried, as Elenna leapt back with a yelp.

"I warned you..." Daltec said,

barely stifling a grin as Elenna eyed the rose crossly. It had settled back into place as if nothing had happened.

Tom got to his feet, glancing warily at the tidy rows of plants all around him. Suddenly, an alarm horn blared from the direction of the palace gate.

Tom frowned. "That sounds like trouble!"

He set off at a run, with Elenna and Daltec close behind him. They sped through the palace gardens, under the stone archway and into the main courtyard. Tom skidded to a stop just as a huge white horse cantered through the palace gates. The creature's heaving sides were flecked with foam. Its rider, a tall knight in full armour, pulled the animal to a halt, then slid from the saddle. He swayed, lifting a hand as if about to

speak, then collapsed to the cobbles with a clatter.

Tom leapt to the fallen warrior's side. He knelt and gently eased off the knight's helmet. Wisps of auburn hair clung to a woman's face, damp with sweat. Her skin looked sunburnt, and a long cut, crusted with dried blood, sliced across one of her cheekbones. Her eyes fluttered open, deep blue, but unfocussed. "Aroha..." she croaked, before slipping back into unconsciousness.

Tom stood at the foot of the wounded soldier's bed, watching as Daltec applied a poultice to the cut on the woman's face. Her armour had been removed, but she had not yet stirred. Apart from the patient's laboured breathing, the infirmary was silent. The quiet was soon broken by the sound of hurrying feet.

"Yara!" cried Queen Aroha, as she burst into the room.

Crossing quickly to the soldier's bedside, the queen took the woman's sunburnt hand in her own. "Yara is one of my most trusted warriors in Tangala," she said, frowning. "She's the personal guard of my nephew, Rotu. Something terrible must have happened for her to come all this way..."

Daltec nodded gravely. "Her

injuries are not life-threatening, but it seems she has ridden for days without rest. The journey has taken its toll."

The woman let out a groan, her face twisting.

"Yara?" Aroha said softly. The warrior's eyes opened. She seemed to flinch back from Aroha's gaze.

"You're in the City," Aroha told her. "You're safe."

Yara shook her head, her forehead creased with anguish. "I'm so sorry, Your Majesty," she said. "I have failed you. Rotu has been kidnapped."

Tom felt a jolt of alarm. He knew the young prince well, and though they had not always seen eye to eye, it was grave news to hear he was in danger.

Aroha gasped. "Kidnapped? By whom?"

"By Zargon, of Vakunda," Yara croaked.

The queen's face drained of colour. "Impossible..." she breathed.

"Who is Zargon?" Tom asked. He had rarely seen the queen look so troubled.

Aroha closed her eyes for a moment. "Zargon was the last wizard of Tangala," she said finally. "More than five hundred years ago, he stole the four Jewels of Tangala and used them to enchant a desert region to the south, called Vakunda.

He created his own kingdom there with four distinct realms – bountiful forests, mountains of gold, a great river and a fertile island paradise where he built a home. Each realm was guarded by a Beast."

Tom's pulse quickened at the mention of Beasts. "Are they still there?" he asked.

Queen Aroha nodded. "I believe so. After only a generation, four Tangalan heroes invaded Vakunda and reclaimed the jewels. Without their magic, Zargon's kingdom changed. The mountains of gold became snow-capped and treacherous, prone to avalanches. The forests grew out of control and the river ran wild, filled with rapids and whirlpools. Even Zargon's island paradise turned upon him, becoming his prison. No Tangalan has dared set foot over the border since, and as far as we knew,

Zargon perished centuries ago."

"He must have used magic to prolong his life," whispered Yara.

"I've never heard of Vakunda before," Daltec said. "It isn't mentioned in any of my history books."

Aroha gave a small sigh. "My people are proud. Once the jewels were hidden, trapping Zargon and his Beasts for ever, there was no need for anyone outside Tangala to know."

"Until now," Elenna said. "But why would this wizard kidnap Rotu?"

Yara let out a grunt of pain as she pushed herself up to sitting, then reached inside her tunic. "Here, Your Majesty," she said, handing a scrap of parchment to the queen.

Aroha scanned the message and gritted her teeth. "Zargon says we must bring him the four jewels," she said. "Otherwise, Rotu dies."

Yara nodded. "We have no choice..."

Queen Aroha shook her head. "Unthinkable!" she snapped. "If Zargon gets the jewels, he will unleash his Beasts on Tangala. He'll have his revenge, and probably kill Rotu anyway. No! I will travel to Vakunda and rescue my nephew!"

Tom and Elenna exchanged a look. "You cannot face four Beasts alone," Tom said. "Elenna and I will come with you."

The queen nodded. "Thank you. But

you will have to get ready quickly."
She lifted her gaze to Daltec. "Please take word to the king. I mean to go at once!"

After Daltec had left, the queen turned back to Yara. "Stay here as long as you need," she said. "Rest and recover. You have done well to bring the news of Rotu's capture so quickly."

"Your Majesty," Yara said, climbing unsteadily from her bed, "this is my fault." She dropped to one knee, her head bowed. "I feel better now my wounds are bound. With your permission, I would like to accompany you too."

Queen Aroha gazed down at Yara and smiled. "I admire your bravery," she said. "If you are sure you are strong enough for the challenge, I gladly accept your offer."

"Thank you, my queen!" Yara stood and crossed the room to fetch her armour. Watching Yara fit her dusty breastplate, Tom felt a rush of admiration for the soldier too. She had barely rested after her long journey but was still eager to serve her queen.

"Tom, please have our horses saddled," Aroha said. "We will meet in the courtyard shortly."

"No need for that," Tom said. The queen raised a questioning eyebrow, and Tom placed a hand on the dragon scale token in his shield. "The journey would take days on horseback," Tom said. "I have a better idea."

A FREEZING FLIGHT

A short while later, their small band stood in the courtyard as Ferno's mighty shadow fell over them.

Thank you for coming so fast, old friend, said Tom, using the red jewel in his belt to communicate his thoughts to the Beast. Yara gave a yelp as the fire dragon's claws thumped on to the ground, and his

massive scaled wings folded. But Queen Aroha, in her own armour, smiled.

“What are we waiting for?” she said.

King Hugo stood to one side, holding baby Thomas. With him were

Aduro and Daltec.

"We will have to travel carefully," Aroha told Tom. "My people are not used to seeing dragons. If they spot Ferno, they will shoot first and ask questions later."

"I have thought of that," Tom said.

"Ferno will fly high, so no one will spot him."

The queen nodded, and Ferno lowered one of his massive wings to the ground. Tom climbed up first, putting out a hand to help the queen. Elenna clambered up next, followed closely by Yara. From the courtyard below, Daltec waved goodbye. Hugo waved too, holding Prince Thomas's small hand in his own.

"Hold on tight!" Tom cried, as with a terrific beat of his massive wings, Ferno powered into the sky. *Time to save Prince Rotu!*

Somewhere far below them, Tom

knew the Ruby Desert stretched from horizon to horizon. But all he could see was cloud as white as a field of snow. Even with his shoulders hunched against the icy wind and his cloak pulled tight about him, he still shuddered with cold. His fingers and toes had long since lost all feeling and his face felt numb and raw.

Tom glanced sideways to see the queen staring grimly ahead, her jaw set. Her skin looked blue. Elenna had wrapped herself deep in her cloak, with only her face peeking from the folds. Yara, huddled at Elenna's side, shivered so hard her armour rattled. Tom felt a stab of pity for the woman. While Aroha had lived in Avantia for long enough to get used to the bitter winters, Yara had probably never felt temperatures like this.

"Take my shield," Tom told her. "Hold it before you. The power of Nanook's bell will warm you."

"Thank...you..." Yara managed, gripping the shield in a trembling hand.

Turning back into the wind, Tom grimaced. Its freezing blast tore at his hair and sliced through his clothes. Even Ferno's scales were covered with a film of slippery frost, making it hard to hold on. *If only I had a shield for each of us...*

As if sensing Tom's discomfort,

Ferno started to blow plumes of fire into the air, trying to warm the passengers on his back. As each fiery blast streamed past above them, Tom felt the fleeting touch of warmth on

his skin – but too soon, it was gone.

"I've been thinking," Elenna shouted over the wind. "If Zargon's trapped on an island surrounded by Beasts, how did he manage to kidnap Rotu?"

Aroha shrugged. "He's had five hundred years to come up with a plan. I suppose he used his evil magic."

"It still seems strange," Elenna said. "Without the jewels, his realm is a prison. How did he break free?"

"What does it matter?" Yara said, crossly. "Rotu's in danger. The most important thing is to rescue him!" Thinking of the young prince trapped by an evil wizard with four

Beasts at his disposal, Tom had to agree.

Suddenly, Yara let out a terrified yelp and slid sideways across Ferno's frosty scales. Elenna grabbed the woman's arm, but the action threw her off balance, and she too slipped across the dragon's frozen hide. A jolt of terror seared through Tom, but somehow, Elenna managed to catch hold of the edge of a scale and stop herself and Yara sliding to their deaths.

"This is no good!" Tom said. "If we stay up here, we'll either freeze to death or fall. Surely we're far enough south to have passed the main cities. Let's go down."

Yara nodded gratefully. Aroha looked troubled, but with her teeth chattering she gave a hesitant nod.

"Let's at least see where we are," the queen said.

Time to head lower, Tom told Ferno, communicating through the red jewel again. The mighty dragon dipped his muzzle, banking downwards. They plunged into swirling whiteness. Cold droplets clung to Tom's hair and skin, then, a moment later, they burst back out into daylight. Tom's heart sank. Graceful spires and sweeping battlements spread below them, along with ornate gardens and courtyards filled with busy market stalls.

"That's Paina!" Aroha called. "We're

too far north! We need to go back up!"

But already Tom could see tiny figures scurrying around on the battlements below, brandishing bows. He heard the blast of a horn. *They've spotted us!* Massive catapults swung around to face them, and huge longbows on scaffolds tipped upwards, taking aim.

Whoosh! A giant bolt sliced the sky a wing's length from Ferno's head. A moment later, a hail of arrows pattered against Ferno's hide.

How dare the tiny folk attack me! the Beast's gruff voice bellowed in Tom's mind. *I'll crush their puny weapons. I'll set fire to their war machines.*

No! Tom told Ferno, speaking to the Beast. *These are Queen Aroha's people. They are afraid.*

"Look out!" Elenna cried, pointing down to where a huge trebuchet had been loaded with a flaming boulder. Tom could feel the rage of the Beast trembling through him.

They want fire? Ferno roared in Tom's mind. *I'll show them fire!*

"No!" Tom shouted. "Rise! Flee!"

But it was too late, as the huge rock slammed into the Beast's jaw from below. Ferno's neck went slack and his head drooped.

"He's out cold!" Tom cried.

Then the dragon's wings folded limply. Tom's stomach flipped as they plummeted towards the city.

FREEFALL

"Ferno! Wake up!" Tom shouted as they plunged closer to the towers and spires below. At his side, Aroha clung to Ferno's scales, her eyes wide with horror.

"We will crush all those people!" she cried. The barrage of arrows had stopped, and Tom could see countless terrified faces gaping up at them as they neared the city walls.

"Can you use Arcta's feather to slow us?" Elenna shouted.

"Good thinking!" Tom said, turning to Yara. "Quick! Give me my shield!" The woman rose to her knees and held the shield out, but before Tom could grab it, she suddenly slipped, tumbling from Ferno's back with a scream.

Tom's gut clenched with horror as he watched Yara plummet. *She has my shield*, he reminded himself. *I can only hope Arcta's feather slows her fall... Now, somehow, I must save the rest of us!* The wind shrieked in Tom's ears as they hurtled faster and faster towards the city.

"We can't die like this!" Aroha said fiercely. "We have to save Rotu!"

Tom swallowed hard, fighting his rising panic. Closing his eyes, Tom touched the red jewel in his belt.

Every nerve in his body screamed with the terrible sensation of falling, but he forced his mind to focus. *Ferno! You must wake, or we will all die!*

Tom could hear cries of terror from the people below, mingled with the howl of the wind. *Ferno! Please!* Suddenly, Tom felt a groggy response from the Beast and a glint of hope kindled inside him.

"Ferno! Fly!" Tom shouted aloud. The Beast's head came up and his fiery eyes opened in alarm. His massive wings unfolding, Ferno slowed with a jolt that almost threw Tom from his back. But already rooftops and battlements sped past right below them, fountains and statues, gardens bright with flowers...

"We're going too fast!" Elenna cried.

Tom angled Ferno towards the biggest open space he could see – a garden with green lawns – then clung with all his strength to the dragon's scales.

"Hold on!" he told the others, bracing. Ferno flung back his wings as they neared the ground, then reached his claws earthwards.

CRASH! The impact thudded through Tom's body, tearing his grip from the dragon's scales. Great clods of mud thrown up by Ferno's claws filled the air as he tumbled. Hurled through the air, Tom tucked his head

and rolled as he landed. Over and over he went until, with a thud that knocked the air from his lungs, his body slammed hard into a tree.

Wincing with pain, Tom clambered

to his feet and looked urgently for the others. Ferno had folded his wings and stood blinking groggily. Nearby, Aroha was shaking her head as if trying to clear dizziness. Elenna was already on her feet, wide-eyed and pale, but unharmed.

Tom let out a sigh of relief. But then he spotted a troop of Tangalan soldiers marching across the grass, their weapons glinting in the sun. Tom gripped the hilt of his sword, but the queen put a hand on his arm.

"Wait," she said, stepping out and shaking out her long, golden hair as she faced the troop. "I am Queen Aroha of Tangala and Avantia," she cried. "Lay down your weapons at once!"

The lead soldier, a powerfully built woman with a jewelled breastplate, drew to a sudden halt, her mouth wide open with shock. Then she saluted. Her soldiers clattered to a stop behind her and quickly followed suit.

"Queen Aroha!" Yara called breathlessly from behind Tom. He turned to see her jogging their way, his shield in her hand. *Arcta's feather must have slowed her fall, as I hoped*, Tom realised with relief.

"Thank goodness you're all safe!" Yara cried.

"No thanks to you," Elenna said

coldly. "Maybe you should give Tom back his shield?"

Yara reddened slightly but handed it over.

Turning back to Aroha, Tom saw the Tangalan soldiers all watching Ferno, their eyes wide with fear. The Beast no longer looked groggy – instead, he glared at the soldiers, pawing the ground with one massive clawed foot. A low growl escaped his scaled snout. Tom hurriedly put a hand to the red jewel in his belt.

You have done Avantia and the queen a great service, he told Ferno. *But it is time for you to go.*

Ferno shot the gathered troops a final, smouldering glare then, sending a puff of flames from his nostrils, stretched his wings and soared into the sky.

With Ferno gone, the Tangalan soldiers all dropped to one knee

before the queen. "Please accept our humblest apologies, Your Majesty," said their leader.

Aroha smiled. "Rise. You could not have expected your queen to fall from the sky on the back of the dragon. You did well, acting quickly to defend the people. Unfortunately, with my nephew missing, I am unable to linger in the capital. I must ask you to prepare chariots to take my companions and me to the border of Vakunda at once."

"I will see to it right away," the woman said.

"Wait!" Yara cut in. "We can't leave yet. We don't have the jewels!"

The queen frowned. "I have no

intention of giving the jewels to Zargon."

"Of course not," Yara said. "But Zargon is a powerful wizard. If he realises we don't have the jewels with us, he might take drastic measures. I have guarded Rotu for many years and could not bear to see him hurt."

Queen Aroha bit her lip. "If we take the jewels, we risk losing them to Zargon," she said.

Elenna looked troubled. "Better to lose the jewels than Prince Rotu's life," she said. "Maybe we should take them, but as a last resort."

"You're right," Queen Aroha said with a sigh. "The jewels are nearby, in a secret vault built by my ancestors. We will fetch them, then head straight to Vakunda."

Tom clung to the small chariot's reins, his feet braced against the juddering floor. Beside him, Yara held tight to the back of the carriage. Not far ahead, the chariot Aroha shared with Elenna bounced along the desert road, sending up puffs of dust. Tom glanced longingly at the sleek, surefooted mares, just as his chariot hit a particularly jolting bump. *Surely it would be more comfortable to ride the horses*, he thought.

To his relief, the queen soon pulled her chariot to a halt alongside a low cliff of red stone. Tom tugged his own horses to a stop and leapt down to join her along with Yara and Elenna. The queen walked slowly

along the cliff-face, looking carefully at the bare rock wall.

"What are you looking for?" Elenna asked.

"Here!" the queen said, gesturing towards the craggy rock. Tom peered

closely to see the faint outline of a circular door. It would have been almost impossible to spot, except that chips of rock had been gouged out around the edge with some sort of tool.

"It looks like someone has tried to break in," Tom said.

Aroha ran her finger over the score marks and nodded. "Zargon, I expect," she said. "But no amount of chiselling or evil magic will open this door. Only the hand of a king or queen of Tangala can unlock it." Aroha lifted her palm and placed it in the centre of the door. For a moment, nothing happened. Then suddenly, Tom heard a hollow *clunk*, followed by a grating rumble as the door rolled aside. He found himself looking into a dark tunnel. A breath of cold, stale air wafted out. Its clammy touch filled him with a sudden dread.

But the queen looked undaunted. "Let's go," she said, stepping inside.

Whumpf!

Tom stared in astonishment and Yara gasped. As Aroha set foot in the passage, a torch on the tunnel wall had flared into life, followed by another, and another, reaching away into the blackness. Tom squared his shoulders, took a deep breath and followed his queen.

THE DEFENDERS

After the desert heat, the shadowy tunnel was cool. Though nothing stirred in the half-darkness, the chill air seemed to prickle with energy.

"It feels like there's someone watching us," Elenna said.

Or something, thought Tom. *The Beasts of Zargon are out there somewhere.*

Queen Aroha turned back, her eyes glinting. "Surely you didn't think my ancestors would leave the jewels unguarded?" she said, then set off with long, purposeful strides. Yara elbowed past Tom and Elenna and hurried to the queen's shoulder. Tom and Elenna followed. Each flaming torch fizzled out as Queen Aroha passed it, leaving Tom and Elenna in shadow. They paced on in silence, the passage darkening behind them, until, when Tom glanced back, the tunnel mouth was only a faint glimmer in the distance.

Finally, the queen stopped, and held up a hand. The passage opened before her into a wide cavern, lit with burning torches set high in the walls. At the back of the chamber stood four life-sized statues of Tangalan female warriors. They had been carved with such detail that despite the rich, red colour of their stone, it was hard to believe they weren't real. They gazed steadily ahead, each with one hand on the hilt of a metal sword, rusted with age, and the other raised palm-upwards, holding a faceted jewel. The four jewels gleamed in the torchlight, each a different colour.

Aroha stood with her head bowed for a moment.

"These brave warriors retrieved the jewels from Zargon five hundred years ago," she said at last. "They agreed to guard the jewels even in death and vowed that only a true ruler of Tangala could take them."

Yara set off across the chamber.

"No!" Aroha cried, but Yara had already reached for a gemstone, the rich, red colour of wine. With a harsh grating sound that made Tom's scalp prickle, the statue's fingers closed on the jewel. At the same moment, the warrior's eyes flared bright, glowing silver. With a rasping hiss that echoed through the chamber, it drew its sword. At the sound, the other three statues jerked to life, their eyes all glowing with the same pale light.

Yara screamed, cowering as the

first statue lunged towards her. Brandishing his weapon, Tom ran past Yara and swung his sword at her attacker's neck. His blade rang as metal bit deep into stone, lodging there and sending a painful shock up his arm. The statue reeled back, tearing the sword from Tom's hand, then toppled, shattering to pieces.

"Watch out!" Elenna cried. Tom turned just in time to meet the gleaming eyes of another statue, lurching towards him. Its fingers shot out, grabbing his throat. A third statue knocked Elenna back with a sweep of its stone fist, but Tom lost sight of his friend as he was slammed against the chamber wall. The statue squeezed his throat and red spots filled his vision. Tom scrabbled at the stone warrior's fingers, trying to pry them from his neck, but its grip tightened. Mustering the last of his

failing strength, Tom drew up both legs and kicked out hard, slamming his feet into the statue's chest. The statue toppled, releasing the pressure on Tom's throat. He fell wheezing to the chamber floor just as the stone warrior burst apart.

Elenna sent her statue sprawling with a high kick to the jaw. It too shattered, but now the final statue was bearing down on Yara, who still cowered on the cavern floor. Before it could reach her, Queen Aroha leapt, and she plunged her blade deep into the stone warrior's heart. The statue froze. Its glowing eyes flickered out, and with a sound like ice shattering, it crumbled to fragments.

In the sudden quiet, Tom found he was shaking, his breath rasping in his aching throat. "They're defeated..." he said. But then a rattling patter from the chamber floor sent a cold finger along his spine. He looked down to see the fractured pieces of statue moving together, merging...re-forming into feet and legs.

"Not for long!" the queen shouted. "Take the jewels and run!" She bent to snatch up a pale blue gem. Tom grabbed the golden jewel at his feet, and Elenna picked a green one from the moving rubble.

"I've got one!" Yara cried, sprinting for the chamber door with

the red jewel in her hand. Queen Aroha raced after her, followed by Elenna. Tom took one last look at the re-forming soldiers, already more than knee high, and bolted after them.

As they raced through the dark passage, the echoing boom of stone footsteps soon joined the clatter of their own. Tom's heart clenched as he remembered the feel of the powerful hand around his throat. He sped onwards, keeping his eyes on the glow at the end of the tunnel. But now he could feel the passage shaking. The thud of the stone warriors' footfalls seemed almost upon them, and the way out impossibly far away. Finally, when he felt like his heart might explode from terror and effort, they burst from the passageway into daylight. Glancing back, Tom saw four sets of glowing eyes in the darkness. Aroha quickly palmed the circular door, and it slammed into place with a boom.

Gasping for breath, Tom sank to the ground. Elenna sat too, panting, while the queen stood with her back to the closed door.

"The ancient defenders have kept their vows well," she said. "Now we have the jewels, we can rescue my nephew."

"I'll look after them," Yara said,

holding out her hand for the queen's jewel.

Elenna scowled. "I think you've caused enough problems. You just almost got us all killed!"

Yara glared at her, but put down her hand. "I couldn't have known that would happen."

"You would have if you'd listened to Aroha!" Elenna snapped. "Only the king or queen of Tangala can take the jewels!"

Tom couldn't help thinking the same. *But it's over now…* "It was just a mistake," he said.

"Exactly!" Yara said.

Queen Aroha lifted a hand. "We don't have time to argue. I will take the jewels." With their heads bowed, Yara and Elenna each handed the queen their jewels. Tom did the same. Aroha slipped the gems into a pouch at her belt and struck off towards her chariot.

As Tom crossed to his own carriage, he knew the queen was right. *Rotu is in danger. We have four Beasts and an evil wizard to overcome. If we are to have any chance of rescuing the prince, and surviving this Quest, we'll have to work as a team.*

DANGER
1

THE LABYRINTH JUNGLE

They travelled without rest across the plains of Tangala, well into the afternoon. Tom ached all over from the constant jolting long before the queen drew her chariot to a halt. But as he stared open-mouthed at the bizarre sight ahead of them, the bone-shaking weariness

evaporated. The grassy plains ended abruptly only paces away, in a wall of dense, tangled jungle. Colossal ferns and bushes with bright, waxy-looking flowers fought for space against vast trees with towering trunks. Great matted loops of vines hung from twisted branches so high above him, it made Tom dizzy to look up. The horses, still yoked to the chariots, whickered in alarm, tugging against their harnesses.

Elenna peered into the shadowy green light under the foliage and frowned. "I've never seen jungle so dense."

"According to the archives it wasn't always like this," Aroha said.

"To start with, it was beautiful and lush, though Zargon kept it all for himself. It was only when the Jewels of Tangala were recovered from Zargon that the trees and plants grew wild."

"Which way do we go?" Elenna asked.

"That's simple," Aroha said, drawing a map from her bag and opening it. Tom and the others leaned in close to see. The map showed a series of circles one inside another, like an archery target. "As long as we travel in a straight line, we will reach the centre, and Zargon's home," Aroha said. The outer circle of the map showed the jungle they stood beside now. *The Labyrinth Jungle*, it read.

The next circle showed a mountain range called The Peaks of Despair. Inside that flowed a circular river, or inland lake, called The Moat of Vakunda. Finally, at the centre, lay an island. *Zargon's Prison*, Tom read. The words *Danger* and *Death* were printed in red beneath a skull and crossbones.

The thought of Rotu held captive in such a place filled Tom with dread. *While there's blood in my veins, we'll set him free!* he vowed.

After stowing her map, Aroha unhitched the horses from their chariots, then clapped her hands. The frightened animals bounded away without a backwards glance. “They’ll return to Tangala,” she said. “Although they are brave and trained for war, nothing would entice them to set foot in this jungle.”

Peering into the murky half-darkness beneath the branches, Tom could see why. The trees, covered in snaking vines and hairy moss, crowded close together as if trying to keep out intruders. Strange contorted plants, some with thorns as long as Tom’s hand, blocked every path he could see.

Tom drew his sword, and led the way into the jungle. Though the

sun still shone high in the sky, only a little light filtered through the dense tree canopy. Tendrils of mist rose from the earth, and Tom soon found it hard to catch his breath in the humid air. He hacked at thorny branches and clinging vines, cutting a way through. Sweat stung his eyes and trickled down his spine. The others followed silently behind him.

Strange smells, some putrid and rotten, others sweet and cloying, caught in Tom's throat. The constant rustle of leaves in the still air made his skin creep. He began to notice strange movements from the corner of his eye – vines twisting like snakes, or boughs swaying when no breeze blew. Branches reached towards him, snagging his clothes and hair. Roots seemed to squirm underfoot as if trying to trip him up. Yet he saw no creatures at all.

"Where are all the animals

and birds?" he whispered to his companions.

"I used to hear tales about this forest when I was young," Aroha said quietly. "Legend says that the trees in this jungle will consume anything or anyone brave or stupid enough to enter."

Yara shuddered. "Then let's get through here quickly!" she said.

Despite the gloom and the ominous rustling all around him, Tom began to see a strange beauty in the unruly tangle of outsized plants. He spotted flowers of every colour and shape he could imagine. And among more sinister scents, he caught pleasant whiffs of honey, rose and sweet fruit.

"Look at this!" Elenna said. Tom turned to see her pointing past him, towards a translucent orb-shaped flower. It had a long green stalk that looked far too slender to support it, and it pulsed with a bright pink light.

Tom edged away from the glowing sphere, eyeing it warily. Then all of a sudden, as Yara caught up with him, the flower exploded, sending out clouds of bright yellow pollen. Yara gasped and started to sneeze, rubbing at her eyes. Though Tom had avoided the worst of the stuff, he could feel his own nose stinging. Elenna and Aroha waited for the cloud to disperse before they continued, but still sneezed and coughed as they passed the flower's sticky remains.

"We should stop for a rest and a drink," Yara said, once they had left the pink flower behind.

"Good idea," Tom said. Even Queen Aroha's steps had grown slow and heavy, and Elenna's short hair was spiky with sweat. They stopped to uncork their water flasks and took long gulps.

As Tom clipped his flask back to his belt, he caught sight of something squirming towards them across the forest floor.

"Look out! A snake!" he cried.

But as the wriggling thing neared Yara, Tom saw it wasn't a snake. *It's a vine!* Yara leapt aside with a cry of alarm as the creeper lashed past her.

Before Tom could act, the striking plant coiled around Queen Aroha's ankle. He watched as she was yanked off her feet and lifted skywards.

THE JUNGLE FIGHTS BACK

Tom's mind raced, trying to think of a way to free the queen as she dangled upside down from a tree branch above him. Elenna let out a shriek. Tom spun to see her shooting upwards, another vine snagged around her leg. He just had time to register a swift movement to his left, before he felt a tight coil whip about his waist. With a painful jerk, his feet left the ground. He managed to hold on to his sword as he flew upwards. An instant later, he found himself hanging beside the queen and Elenna. Yara looked up at them, her blue eyes wide.

"What do I do?" she called.

Tom slashed at the vine that squeezed his middle, severing it. Landing in a crouch on the forest floor, Tom looked up to see the queen swing her own blade for the vine around her foot. But another green shoot snapped closed around her sword-arm, yanking it out to the side before her blow could land.

"Hold still," Elenna called to Aroha. Tom saw that even dangling upside down, Elenna had freed her bow and aimed an arrow at the vine trapping Aroha's wrist. *Twang!* Elenna's arrow sliced through the tendril. Without wasting a second, Aroha bent double and swung her sword, severing the creeper that held her ankle. She flipped in the air and landed lightly beside Tom.

Gripping the vine with her free hand, Elenna let her bow fall to the ground, then reached to use an arrow-head to cut through the vine holding her. Free of its grip, she swung on the vine across to the tree trunk and then quickly shimmied down the branches to the ground.

"This is worse than Daltec's garden!" Elenna said. "Let's go, quickly!" But the queen let out a cry of dismay and shook her head.

"The jewels!" Aroha clutched the empty pouch at her side. "They must have fallen!" She dropped to her knees and started searching frantically among the roots and ferns. Tom and Elenna did the same, but Yara let out a scream.

"There are more vines coming!" she cried.

Tom leapt up to see what looked like dozens of green tendrils snaking across the ground towards them. Horror churning inside him, he lifted his sword and started to hack at the shoots. "Keep searching for the jewels!" he told the others.

Tom slashed and chopped at the moving forest floor, tearing through clumps of slithering vegetation, desperate to keep them from reaching his friends. His arm soon ached, but more shoots came.

"Aroha!" he cried. "I need your help!"

The queen sprang to his side, joining the battle against the encroaching plants. But though they both sliced through scores of vines with each stroke, the creepers kept coming.

One coiled up the queen's armoured leg and tugged, making her stagger. Tom quickly cut it free, but another vine snatched at his

arm. Aroha sliced through it, but when her eyes met Tom's they were full of desperation. "We must flee, or we will all be caught by the jungle and perish!"

"Go! Now!" Elenna shouted. Tom turned to see Elenna already running, Yara racing ahead of her. Aroha sprang away too.

The jewels! Tom thought. More creepers slithered through the undergrowth – too many to count. His heart heavy with dread, Tom took off after the queen.

Their footsteps pounded over the forest floor as they vaulted roots and ducked under branches. Thorns tore at Tom's clothes and face, but he plunged on, his breath ragged and his skin slick with sweat. Still he heard the slithering rasp of clutching greenery.

Finally, they reached an open, grassy glade. Elenna turned, holding up a hand for quiet. They stopped and listened. Apart from the sound of their heaving breath, the clearing was silent.

"We've lost the vines..." Elenna murmured, sinking on to the grass and closing her eyes with relief.

"But the jewels of my people!" Queen Aroha cried. "They're gone. What if they get into the hands of Zargon?"

Elenna opened her eyes. She frowned. "Yara has them," she said. "She found them on the ground. That's why I said to run."

The queen turned to her

countrywoman, her face bright with hope. "Yara?" she asked.

Tom saw Yara blushing. She reached into her tunic and drew out the gems. "Your Majesty," she said, handing them to the queen. "I am

honoured to be able to return the jewels."

"Thank you!" Aroha said, tucking them back into her pouch.

Suddenly a loud snort sounded through the clearing. Tom spun to see the trees on the far side of the dell swaying violently. More snaps and crashes filled the air.

"Something's coming!" Tom said. "Hide!" They ducked back into the jungle, hidden behind the thick foliage, as a rancid, animal stink rolled over Tom, snatching his breath away. A moment later, massive hands with gnarled yellow claws reached through the trembling bushes opposite them.

“Akorta...” Aroha breathed, her voice edged with fear.

A Beast, Tom thought, as a huge shaggy head thrust into view. A single yellow, bloodshot eye scanned the clearing. Tom recognised the features of an ape…but the Beast's head alone was the size of an ox. His lips spread into a wide grimace, showing jagged, blackened teeth. Tom tightened his grip on the hilt of his sword, his heart hammering. *It hasn't seen us…*

Crack! Yara tripped over a rotten branch and fell on her backside with a clang of armour.

The huge ape froze. His evil grin spread wider. Then with a snarl of rage, he leapt into the open.

AKORTA ATTACKS

Tom stared in horror from his hiding place as the Beast landed with a thud that shook the ground, then stood with his huge eye fixed on their small group. As he stood upright on his bowed hind legs, Akorta's head reached almost to the treetops. Muscles bulged in his long, rangy limbs, and his ribs poked

through bald patches in the matted fur that covered his barrel chest. Yara scrambled to her feet and backed into the cover of the leafy bushes.

Akorta let out a furious snort, then tore a sapling from the earth and lifted it high, brandishing it like a club. His single eye glared into the undergrowth where Yara cowered, and he let out a bellow of rage.

"I'm going to try and sneak up on him," Tom hissed to Elenna and Aroha. "Be ready to run for it." Without waiting for an answer, Tom dropped into a crouch and skirted around the edge of the glade. He trod carefully, avoiding the scattered twigs and leaves until the Beast's massive, ungainly form towered before him.

Up close, the rotting stench of the giant ape made Tom gasp. He lifted his sword and took aim at the creature's muscular leg. But before he could strike, another red-rimmed eye snapped open in the back of Akorta's head, swivelling downwards to glare straight at Tom. Terror fizzed through him as the giant ape spun with monstrous speed and brought his club smashing towards Tom's head. Tom threw himself down, rolling under the shelter of a nearby tree root.

CRASH! The ground leapt. Twigs and splintered wood pattered against Tom's hiding place.

"ROOOOAAAAR!" Drool sprayed from Akorta's jaws, and with a snort of disgust he threw down the sapling he held. An instant later, Tom felt the smaller roots crack and snap around him. Stones and earth rained down as Akorta wrenched the tree protecting Tom from the ground.

Exposed, Tom stared up past Akorta's heaving chest and into the ape's bulging yellow eye. Flaring his nostrils, Akorta raised the tree, ready to smash Tom flat.

Tom reached desperately for the

magic red jewel in his belt.

Akorta, wait! We mean you no harm!

But as Tom's mind touched that of the Beast, the only feelings he could sense were the same terrible rage and all-consuming hunger he'd seen in the creature's eye. With a grunt, Akorta sent the mighty cudgel crashing towards him. With nowhere to run, Tom braced his muscles, knowing it wouldn't be enough…

Somehow, the blow fell wide. Letting out a strangled bellow of rage, Akorta spun, the tree falling from his hand and crashing to the ground. Tom spotted Elenna's arrow lodged in the sparse hair of his back. And with a rush of relief, he saw his three companions through the Beast's bowed legs.

Tom started to scramble up, but Akorta lifted a mighty foot and stamped. The jungle floor shook, sending Tom sprawling once more. On the far side of the clearing Tom's friends all tumbled too. With a hungry, slavering snort, Akorta lunged towards them.

I must strike quickly, or he'll kill them all! Tom staggered up and threw himself towards the Beast, swinging his sword for the thick tendons at the back of Akorta's foot just as the huge eye on the back of

Akorta's head locked on to Tom. The Beast lifted his colossal foot and stomped backwards, right for Tom.

Tom dived, throwing himself as far as he could.

BOOM! The Beast's foot slammed down, missing Tom by a hand's breadth.

Tom rolled and shrank back, expecting the Beast to stomp again, but Elenna was on her feet, firing an arrow that lodged in the ape's knee. Akorta bellowed with pain. Now, Tom could see Aroha had risen to stand with Elenna, but Yara still lay on the ground, motionless.

Did the Beast strike her? Or is she playing dead?

"Tom! Elenna! Keep Akorta busy!" Aroha shouted, then dashed towards the edge of the clearing.

Elenna let another arrow fly. It struck Akorta square in the chest. With a bellow of anger, the Beast pulled the dart from his flesh and tossed it away. Elenna ran. The Beast lurched after her, heading away from the queen. Tom took the chance Elenna had given him. He lunged, swiping his sword at Akorta's legs. He just managed to rake the tip of his blade across the creature's sinewy calf, but it didn't slow the Beast. Tom slashed again at Akorta's leg, and again. Elenna raced onwards before the Beast, firing arrows back at him. Attacked from both sides, the Beast roared, sending spittle flying, then swiped out madly with his huge fists. Tom ducked just before one swatted him like a bug. Elenna leapt sideways, narrowly missing being crushed by the other.

Looking frantically for Aroha, Tom spotted her scrambling up a tree. *She's going to attack from above!* Tom realised. *It might work! But only if we can keep Akorta's eyes on the ground.* Tom glanced back to see the ravenous Beast grabbing for Elenna with both hands. From almost point-blank range, Elenna fired. *Thwack!* Tom winced as her arrow struck, sticking beneath one of Akorta's yellow nails.

With a roar of agony, Akorta reared, cradling his injured hand,

then plucked the arrow free and
flung it away. Tom could see
Aroha balanced on a long branch

overhanging the glade. He gasped in wonder as she leapt, her sword lifted high, straight for Akorta's shaggy head. *She's got him!* But Tom's elation turned quickly to horror. Akorta's jaws spread into a grin, and his mighty hand reached behind him to pluck the queen from the air.

Aroha let out a strangled cry as hairy fingers closed tight around her. Her sword tumbled from her grip. Tom watched, horror coursing through him, as Akorta opened his enormous mouth, ready to eat the queen!

BLOOD-RED MIST

Time seemed to stand still as Akorta lowered the queen towards his blackened teeth. *I'm too far away!* Tom realised. He considered throwing his sword, but knew it would barely pierce Akorta's hide, let alone stop him.

Suddenly, Elenna crouched, snatching something pink and

gleaming from the ground. She flung it hard, right at Akorta's forward-facing eye. As the pink object struck the Beast's face, it exploded, sending out a yellow cloud. *Pollen!* Tom realised. The Beast blinked hard and let out a

shuddering sneeze. Akorta bent double, coughing, but still kept a tight grip on the queen. Aroha's face was twisted with agony, and she looked deathly pale.

Tom scanned the ground in desperation, spotting a length of rope-like vine. He snatched it, ducked his head and raced towards the Beast. Hurling himself at the matted fur of Akorta's leg, Tom clung tight and scrambled up the Beast's back.

I am here! Tom cried to the Beast, calling on the power of the red jewel in his belt. *I am the Master of the Beasts and I will not let you harm my queen!* Clambering until he reached the Beast's massive shoulders, Tom drove his sword into the flesh of Akorta's neck. With a snort of pain, the Beast dropped Aroha and reached instead for Tom. Scrambling quickly out of reach, Tom looped the vine in a tight lasso around the Beast's neck, then threw himself off, still holding the end. He landed with a thud behind Akorta, then heaved on his makeshift garrote.

The Beast stumbled back, reaching for his throat. His huge foot caught on a log, and he toppled, landing with an earth-shaking crash.

"Help me!" Tom cried to Elenna

and Aroha, tugging on the vine with both hands. A moment later, Elenna reached him, then Aroha, still wincing and gasping for breath. They gripped the vine alongside Tom and the three of them pulled, using every fibre of their strength.

Akorta writhed, shaking his head from side to side. Tom braced his muscles and dug his heels into the ground. Aroha let out a furious cry as she heaved, and Elenna groaned with effort but somehow, they all kept their grip on the vine and pulled harder still. Akorta let out a strangled growl. His huge eye bulged, and his tongue lolled from

between his rotten teeth. Calling on the magical strength of his golden breastplate, Tom gave the vine lasso one final, mighty tug.

With a hiss of putrid breath, the Beast fell still. His massive eye swivelled wildly for an instant, then finally closed.

"He's defeated!" Tom said, letting the lasso fall. Elenna and Aroha did the same. Gazing at the giant body of the fallen ape, Tom suddenly felt weary and sick. Aroha and Elenna fell to their knees, and Tom spotted a red light pulsing through the fabric of the pouch the queen wore.

"What's that?" he asked.

Queen Aroha stood and drew out the red royal Jewel of Tangala, which now shone with a ruby light. As she lifted the glowing gem, the Beast's gigantic, hairy body seemed to collapse inwards with a sigh. A moment later, it dissolved into a cloud of swirling red smoke which streamed into the jewel. The jewel glowed brighter for an instant as the last of the deep red mist flowed into it, then turned dark.

"Of course!" said the queen. "The

jewels gave the Beast life, and now they take back its spirit."

A creaking, whispering sound started up, coming from all around them. For a panicked moment, Tom feared another Beast was coming,

but as he glanced around, he saw it was something quite different. The massive trees were actually shrinking, the outsized ferns coiling in on themselves. He blinked, feeling almost as if he were waking from a dream. In a matter of a few heartbeats, the Labyrinth Jungle had become nothing more than a lush, leafy forest. Somewhere, far in the distance, Tom heard the trill of a bird.

Elenna gazed about, her eyes wide with amazement. "This must be how the forest was long ago, when Zargon created it with the jewels."

"I think you're right," Aroha said, her face lit with wonder, but then her expression turned to alarm. "Yara!" she cried, jogging towards the young woman, who lay still in the shadow of a bush. Tom raced to the queen's side, his hand already reaching for the green jewel of healing in his belt.

Aroha shook Yara's shoulder. The woman stirred, then struggled to her feet. "What happened?" Yara asked, rubbing her temple. "I must have hit my head during the fighting… Oh! The Beast's gone! And the forest – it's different… You did it! You defeated Akorta!"

"Indeed we did," Queen Aroha said, her voice sounding weary and grim. "Thanks to Tom and

Elenna. But before we can rescue Rotu, there are three more Beasts to defeat. Not to mention Zargon himself."

Tom stood up tall and squared his aching shoulders. Elenna and the queen both looked as battered and exhausted as he felt, and Tom knew they could all do with a rest before they faced another Beast. *But a Quest never waits*, he thought, *and this one has only just begun*.

THE END

CONGRATULATIONS, YOU HAVE COMPLETED THIS QUEST!

At the end of each chapter you were awarded a special gold coin. The QUEST in this book was worth an amazing 8 coins.

Look at the Beast Quest totem picture opposite to see how far you've come in your journey to become

MASTER OF THE BEASTS.

The more books you read, the more coins you will collect!

Do you want your own Beast Quest Totem?

1. Cut out and collect the coin below
2. Go to the Beast Quest website
3. Download and print out your totem
4. Add your coin to the totem

www.beastquest.co.uk

READ THE BOOKS, COLLECT THE COINS!

EARN COINS FOR EVERY CHAPTER YOU READ!

550+ COINS
MASTER OF THE BEASTS

410 COINS
HERO

350 COINS
WARRIOR

230 COINS
KNIGHT

180 COINS
SQUIRE

44 COINS
PAGE

8 COINS
APPRENTICE

550+
515
480
445
410
395
380
365
350
320
290
260
230
217
206
191
180
146
112
78
44
30
19
8

READ ALL THE BOOKS IN SERIES 25:

THE PRISON KINGDOM!

Don't miss the next exciting Beast Quest book: LYCAXA, HUNTER OF THE PEAKS!

Read on for a sneak peek...

ZARGON RETURNS

Tom gazed about in wonder at the lush undergrowth as he and Elenna trudged through the Labyrinth Jungle. Queen Aroha walked ahead of them with Yara, one of her most trusted warriors. Morning sunlight cast golden shafts through mist rising from the earth all around them. Its warmth eased Tom's muscles, stiff from a night spent sleeping on the ground. Colourful butterflies and tiny birds, no bigger than bees, flitted between flowers, and silver-blue fish splashed in the babbling stream at their side. Tom plucked a peach from a low-hanging branch and sank his teeth into its sweet golden flesh.

"This is good!" he said, wiping juice from his chin.

Elenna popped the last grape from the bunch she'd been eating into her mouth. "When it's not trying to kill us, Vakunda's a paradise!" she said once she'd finished. "Maybe the whole of the kingdom will be as beautiful as this after we've defeated the other three Beasts that guard it."

"We can only hope so," Queen Aroha said, hurrying onwards without looking back. "But remember, we're here to find Rotu, and bring him home alive."

Tom, Elenna and the queen had already battled Akorta, a giant ape-Beast, on the first stage of their Quest to rescue Aroha's nephew from the Evil Wizard, Zargon. Upon the Beast's demise, the overgrown jungle of Zargon's cursed kingdom had begun to transform. Trees, which only yesterday had been tangled with snaking vines, were now bowed beneath the weight of ripe fruit. Their once silent branches rustled with life.

"Personally, I can't wait to get out of here," Yara muttered, swatting at a mosquito. The Tangalan warrior had been Prince Rotu's bodyguard at the time of his capture and had volunteered to help with his rescue. "If it isn't an outsized monkey trying to eat us alive, it's the insects!"

Tom finished his peach and stooped to rinse his sticky hands in the cool water of the stream. He rose to join the others as they walked through a leafy curtain of vegetation and stopped in the bright sunshine of a grassy plain.

Once Tom's eyes had adjusted, his spirits plummeted. An immense mountain range spanned the horizon, climbing in a series of jagged peaks to blade-like summits that jutted into the clear blue sky.

"The Peaks of Despair," Queen Aroha said. "They used to be known as the Hills of Plenty, but they changed when the Jewels of Tangala were taken back from Zargon. No one has set foot on these mountains for five hundred years."

"I'm not sure we should chance our luck either," Elenna said, frowning up at the snow-capped peaks. "We've only got one rope. Is there any way around them?"

"Perhaps you should return to Avantia..." Yara said, scowling, "...if you're *afraid*."

Elenna rounded on the woman, her cheeks flushing as if she'd been slapped.

"There's no point risking our necks if we don't have to," she said. "After all, if we fall to our deaths, there won't be anyone left to save Prince Rotu."

Her eyes cold and hard, Yara opened her mouth to speak, but Aroha cut her off.

"Peace!" the queen said, sharply. "Crossing the mountains will be dangerous. But look..." She opened her map and gestured to a ring of mountains surrounded by a jungle. "Just like the Labyrinth Jungle, they form a ring. The only way to get to Zargon's island at the centre is to climb. And we will have to work together if we mean to reach the other side alive."

Yara quickly bowed her head. "Of course, my queen," she said.

"I'm sorry, Your Majesty," Elenna muttered, her cheeks glowing even redder.

Queen Aroha turned on her heel and struck off towards the mountains. Tom started after her, but a sudden flash of white light made him reel back, blinded. He blinked hard to find the shimmering image of a tall, muscular man clad in black wizard's robes standing before them, his tanned, bare arms folded across his chest. A clipped beard and moustache surrounded his thin lips, which were drawn back in a sneer of distaste. His curled hair showed no hint of white and his skin was smooth, but somehow his hooded grey eyes looked as old and as uncaring as mountains themselves. As Tom met the wizard's pitiless gaze, he suppressed a shudder. It felt like staring into the eyes of a venomous snake.

"Zargon!" Aroha gasped, flinching back from the vision, but then she drew herself tall. "Where is Rotu?"

she demanded.

A smile played at the corners of the wizard's lips. "He is safe. For now…" he said, then lifted a black-gloved hand, turning it towards the sun so that a gold ring worn over the leather caught the light.

"That's Rotu's!" Aroha cried.

Read

LYCAXA, HUNTER OF THE PEAKS

to find out what happens next!

Meet three new heroes with the power to tame the Beasts!

MEET TEAM HERO
FROM ADAM BLADE
THEIR GIFTS MAKE THEM DIFFERENT
NICE HANDS!
FREAK!
BUT WHEN DANGER COMES...
CRACK!
RUMBLE!
SCREEECH!
...A HERO IS BORN
OTHERS WITH GIFTS WILL SEEK THEM OUT...
...AND SHOW THEM THEIR DESTINY.
EVER HEARD OF HERO ACADEMY?
OUT NOW!
ADAM BLADE
TEAM HERO
BATTLE FOR THE SHADOW SWORD
ADAM BLADE
TEAM HERO
ATTACK OF THE BAT ARMY
ADAM BLADE
TEAM HERO
REPTILE REAWAKENED
ADAM BLADE
TEAM HERO
THE SKELETON WARRIOR
31901066048499
DARE TO BE DIFFERENT